W9-BRS-717

DENNIS HASELEY
A STORY FOR BEAR

Illustrated by

JIM LaMARCHE

SILVER WHISTLE
HARCOURT, INC.
San Diego   New York   London

For Connor

—D. H.

For Paula

—J. L. M.

Library of Congress Cataloging-in-Publication Data
Haseley, Dennis.
A story for bear/Dennis Haseley; illustrated by Jim LaMarche.
p.   cm.
"Silver Whistle."
Summary: A young bear who is fascinated by the mysterious marks he sees on paper finds a friend when a kind woman reads to him.
[1. Literacy—Fiction.   2. Books and reading—Fiction.   3. Bears—Fiction.]   I. LaMarche, Jim, ill.   II. Title.
PZ7.H2688St   2002
[E]—dc21   2001002141
ISBN 0-15-200239-1

G H

Manufactured in China

The illustrations in this book were done in acrylic paint and colored pencil on Arches watercolor paper.
The display type was set in Powhatten.
The text type was set in Adobe Jenson.
Color separations by Colourscan Co. Pte. Ltd., Singapore
Manufactured by South China Printing Company, Ltd., China
This book was printed on totally chlorine-free Nymolla Matte Art paper.
Production supervision by Sandra Grebenar and Pascha Gerlinger
Designed by Linda Lockowitz

One day, a young bear was nosing through
bushes when he saw something lying on the ground.

He looked at it with curiosity. He sniffed at its
tiny marks. Then the bear took it in his teeth and
brought it back to his cave.

Through the years, the bear looked at the paper with wonder—it seemed as far away and mysterious as the moon.

One summer afternoon, the bear ranged farther than usual from where he lived. He followed a scent until he came to a clearing, and there he saw several strange things all at once. There was a cabin, and brightly colored laundry hanging on a line, and a woman.

From behind a thick tree, he watched as the woman sat down and opened a mysterious square thing she was carrying. His nose tickled from the wonderful smells of the cabin—bacon and coffee and bread—but he gazed only at her, trying to understand what she was doing as she held the book.

He felt calm as he watched her.

When she closed the book, he ran away.

Day after day, he returned.

He managed to get closer to her, and watched from behind a near tree, his thick bear head just peeking around. He had never seen anything like this.

Sometimes, as she gazed at the book, she laughed out loud.

Other times, she lowered it and looked away, but without really seeing anything, he thought.

Still other times, she appeared afraid and held it tightly. And once, when the sun slanted through the trees, he saw her place it gently on her lap and close her eyes.

Later, she went into her cabin, and he lumbered slowly through the woods back to his cave. When he heard a blue jay call, he looked up quickly, because he thought for a moment it was the woman laughing.

One afternoon, the woman was not in her yard. Slowly, his head moving from side to side, he walked toward her things.

With one big paw, he knocked a book off the pile, to land facedown in the dirt. He pushed it with his nose and scratched at its brown cover with his claws, trying to turn it over.

Finally, one of his claws caught under the cover, and the book flipped over, opened—the bear moved his nose forward—then it closed again, and his head snapped back. Once more he tried, and this time it stayed open. He took two lumbering steps toward it, and put his big head close.

There on the page were row after row of marks, tiny marks, like those on the piece of paper in his cave. He stared at them, while his nose filled with the scents of paper, glue, ink, and her touch. He didn't see the woman walking up behind him. When he finally heard her, his head swung around.

For a moment, their eyes locked. The bear pawed once more at the book, then turned and ran away.

The next day, he saw the woman sitting in her chair, the book with the brown cover on her lap. She was looking into the trees, searching for something. When she finally saw him, she smiled.

"Come here. Come here, bear."

After a while, he moved out from the tree, and then slowly he took a few steps toward her, with his big head swaying from side to side.

When he grew near to her—but not so near
that he couldn't run—he lay down and looked up at
her. She waited a moment longer. Then she carefully
opened the book, and softly she began to speak.

"There once was a sailor," she read, "who had to
travel for many years over the sea before he could
return home."

The bear gazed up at her as she said the words
and turned the pages. He couldn't understand any of
what she was saying. But as he listened to the sound
of her voice, happiness washed over him like waves.

He returned, day after day, all that summer. When she read in a fearful voice about the sailor getting lost, he felt afraid. When she laughed at how the sailor played tricks, the bear would feel strangely happy. When she read of his love, the bear looked up at the woman with wide eyes and watched as her gentle mouth formed the words.

All the words she read made a story.

A story for her bear.

Whenever she read, he felt the waves of mysterious feelings carried by her voice. Sometimes her voice was soothing and the bear grew peaceful; and sometimes she sounded excited or scared and his hair bristled and he gave a low growl; and sometimes her sounds were tender and he looked up at her and watched her fingers gently lifting a page, and a page, and a page. These feelings often stayed inside of him as he lumbered back to his world at the end of the day; and sometimes, in the babbling of a brook, he would think he heard her again and become quite happy.

One afternoon, when he returned to the cabin, there was a chill in the air. She put down her book, looked at the bear, and said, "I wish … Oh, I wish you could read these books when I'm away for the winter." Then she smiled at him, and the bear, seeing her smile, felt lightness in his heart.

And she began to read aloud again.

When next he came, he was carrying something in his mouth. It was the scrap of paper from his cave, with its mysterious marks. He laid it by her books.

"Bear?" she said. He knew by now that this was her word for him, and he lifted his head. "Bear, did you bring this for me?"

And then she read it in her gentle voice, as if it were a story he was giving to her.

Dear Eliza,
Your father and I have been cheered by your letter.
We picture you often, living near the woods where
we summered. I remember days of berry picking
and golden light shining through tall trees...

When the bear next returned, the leaves were changing color. When he reached the cabin, he saw what had changed there as well.

She was not in her usual place, waiting for him. The bear walked into her yard, taking a few steps and moving his big head from side to side. He walked this way up to where her chair had been.

There, under the tree where she usually sat, were her books. There were many of them, more than he had ever seen, lying on a cloth, fallen leaves and pinecones on their covers.

She had left them for him, along with a piece of paper—as if she'd wished he could read it.

For my Bear

He looked at what she'd left him, with his big head close. He understood that she had gone, as silence surrounded him.

Then, tenderly, as tenderly as he could, he put his teeth around the book with the brown cover, and carried it away.

All that afternoon, he made the long journey from his winter cave to her yard, and back again through the forest—carrying her books with their covers of green and red and black, their words of sailors and goddesses and far-off lands—while the stream whispered and the blue jays called.

That night, as the moon rose like a white page with mysterious marks, he lay among the hard covers of her books.

Finally, he slept.

And while he slept, he heard her voice, gentle and near. She was telling him a tale of adventure, and magic, and love.

And all that winter, before she came back in the spring, whenever he put his nose to the pages or touched the covers with his claws, she was there …

reading to him.